To my mother, with love. —J. S.

To Henry Lyman and Toshi Seeger, with gratitude. —P. J.

To my extraordinary father, with my everlasting gratitude for teaching me how to paint and encouraging me to follow my dreams. —S. A.

First Edition
10 09 08 07 06 5 4 3 2 1

Text © 2006 Jacobs and Swender, Inc.
Illustrations © 2006 Selina Alko

Published by
Gibbs Smith, Publisher
P.O. Box 667
Layton, Utah 84041

Orders: 1.800.748.5439
www.gibbs-smith.com

Designed by Dawn DeVries Sokol
Printed and bound in Hong Kong

Library of Congress Cataloging-in-Publication Data

Jacobs, Paul DuBois.
    My taxi ride / Paul DuBois Jacobs and Jennifer Swender ; illustrations by Selina Alko. — 1st ed.
        p. cm.
    Summary: Illustrations and rhythmic text describe the sights and sounds of a taxi ride in New York City.
    ISBN 1-4236-0073-8
    [1. Taxicabs—Fiction. 2. New York (N.Y.)—Fiction. 3. Stories in rhyme.]   I. Swender, Jennifer. II. Alko, Selina, ill. III. Title.
PZ8.3.J1383My 2006
[E]—dc22

2006003658

My TAXi Ride

**PAUL DUBOIS JACOBS
AND JENNIFER SWENDER**

Illustrations by Selina Alko

Gibbs Smith, Publisher
Salt Lake City

Hail taxi! Hey taxi!
Ho taxi! Yo taxi!

Where to, Miss? Where to, Mister?
Where to, Brother? Where to, Sister?

All around our New York town!

A bus is fine, but it sticks to a line.
That's okay if you've got the time.
A train is a treat, but it's stuck on a track.
That's a drag if you're late to get back.
A car is quick but you've got to park it.
A bike is cool but you've got to lock it.

In a rush? No time to spare?
Hail a cab to take you there.
To the store or to the theater,
Just keep one eye on the meter.

As long as you have got the fare,
New York cabs go anywhere!
Anywhere you need to be—
Directly from point A to B.

Is a taxi red or green?
Not in this Big Apple scene.
A yellow cab is easy to see,
Buzzin' around like a bumblebee.
Now you know that you can spot one,
Next step is to try to stop one!
It's a breeze. Nothin' to it.
Find a curb. Here's how to do it.

Raise your arm and point your finger.
Belt it out like an opera singer:
Hail taxi! Hey taxi!
Ho taxi! Yo taxi! WHOA TAXI!

That cab wasn't being snooty.
Read the letters, it's OFF DUTY.

Don't despair. Here comes another.
(More than 12,000 all together!)
Step on up and don't be shy.
Shout to the rooftops. Shout to the sky:
Hail taxi! Hey taxi!
Ho taxi! Yo taxi! HELLO TAXI!

Get on in. Scoot on over.
Seat belts on. Time to motor!

Three in the back and one in the front,
Driver at the wheel and bags in the trunk.

Where to, Miss? Where to, Mister?
Where to, Brother? Where to, Sister?

Tell the cabbie where you need
  to go,
But don't forget to say "hello."
(And "please" and "thank you,"
  don't you know.)

Hola, I'm from Mexico.
Preevyet, I'm from old Moscow.
We say *Adaab* in Pakistan.
We say *Xin chào* in Vietnam.
In Czech Republic, it's *Dobrý den*.
In New York City, it's *How ya doin'?*

From the Lower East to the Upper West,
Ride to the Side you like the best.
From Washington Heights to Brooklyn Heights,
Climb on in and see the sights.
MOMA! SOHO! NOHO! DUMBO!
All around our New York town!
We might go fast. We might go slow.
Ready or not, here we go!

Duck a truck and horns go HONK.
Ride it like a bucking bronc.
Weave and wave and "That was close, sir!"
Ride it like a rollercoaster.
Hey taxi! Ho taxi!
Whoa taxi! SLOW TAXI!

Horns go BEEP! And horns go BAM!
Man, oh, man, a TRAFFIC JAM!

Soon enough we start to move.
Now we're really in the groove.
First stop is the Great White Way.
See a musical. Catch a play.
We've got tickets to a matinee.
Stop the cab on Old Broadway!

Next stop on this New York trip—
Greenwich Village, if you're hip.
Winding through the narrow streets,
Lots of yummy things to eat.
At a jazz club hear the beat.
Stop the cab at Bleecker Street!

Now to a building that's ideal.
Made of stone and made of steel.
From the top the view is great.
Seventy-three elevators (plus six freight).
Called World Wonder Number 8.
Stop the cab at the Empire State!

Next a spot to make you smile.
Its eastern edge is Museum Mile.
With saffron Gates and Tavern green,
The biggest park you've ever seen.
The Zoo is zen. The Rink is cool.
The Lawn, the Mall, the Pond, the Pool.
Where bikers bike and doggies bark,
Stop the cab at Central Park!

We sure did ramble, sure did roam.
Now it's time to head for home.
Check the meter. Pay the fare.
Exit curbside with great care.
Tip the driver. Tip your hat.
Say good-bye and that is that.

That is till the next go-round,
Next time when we sing the sound:

Hail taxi! Hey taxi!
Ho taxi! Yo taxi!

Where to, Miss? Where to, Mister?
Where to, Brother? Where to, Sister?

All around our New York town!